THE FAIRIES'
SHOEMAKER
AND OTHER STORIES

The Fairies' Shoemaker

and Other Stories

by
ENID BLYTON

Illustrated by
Sally Gregory

AWARD PUBLICATIONS

ISBN 0-86163-180-3

Text copyright 1928, 1943, 1945 Darrell Waters Limited
Illustrations copyright © 1987 Award Publications Limited

Enid Blyton's signature is a trademark of Darrell Waters Limited

This edition contains extracts from *Pinkity's Pranks and Other Nature
Fairy Tales* first published 1928 by Thomas Nelson and Sons, Limited; *Enid Blyton's Merry Story Book* first published 1943 by Brock-
hampton Press Limited; *The Conjuring Wizard and Other Stories* first
published 1945 by Macmillan and Co. Limited

This edition entiled *The Fairies' Shoemaker and Other Stories*
First published 1987
6th impression 1993

Published by Award Publications Limited,
Spring House, Spring Place, London NW5 3BH

Printed in Hungary

CONTENTS

1

Pinkity's Pranks

Once upon a time there lived a naughty little pixie called Pinkity. He was always in mischief, and teased every one he met.

'Now, what shall I do today?' thought Pinkity, as he sat in a may-bush and swung his legs. 'I know – I'll get my little watering-can and water all the people who walk in the wood!'

He flew to get it, and filled it with water. Then he perched himself up in his tree again and waited.

Presently along came Dwarf Yellow Buttons, carrying his lovely new mackintosh, and walked just underneath Pinkity's tree.

Splish-splash! splish-splash!

Down went the water from Pinkity's

can, all over Dwarf Yellow Buttons!

'Dear, dear, dear!' cried Dwarf Yellow Buttons, hastily putting on his mackintosh. 'Who would have thought it would rain so soon?'

Pinkity laughed and laughed to see Yellow Buttons running off into the sunshine with his mackintosh on!

Presently came the Lord High Chancellor of Fairyland, talking earnestly with the Prince of Dreamland.

Splish-splash! splish-splash!

Down came the water over them!

'Why bless me!' cried the Chancellor, hurriedly putting up a large red umbrella. 'Fancy it raining like this! I hope you're not wet, your Highness!'

'Yes, I am,' said the Prince; 'and I don't believe it's rain, I believe it's a trick. See, the sun is shining yonder!'

Then the Chancellor heard Pinkity laughing, and he looked up into the may-bush.

'You bad, mischievous little pixie!' he cried, in a great rage. 'I'll catch you and take you to the King.'

But Pinkity flew off in a great hurry, and was soon lost to sight. He was just a bit frightened, and for a little while he was quite good.

He wandered over the fields, and suddenly saw some one lying down fast asleep, and snoring, by the hedge.

He crept up to look.

'It's old Togs the Tailor!' he said to himself, in great delight. 'I'll borrow his big scissors for a little while.'

So Pinkity took the tailor's scissors, and flew off with them, looking for something to cut and snip.

Now in the next field were a lot of fairy sheep with their little lambs.

'Hullo!' said Pinkity, flying up to

them; 'look what I've got! Old Togs the Tailor's scissors!'

'Oh, Pinkity, *do* cut off our heavy tails!' begged the lambs, crowding round him. 'They're so hot, and they knock against our legs so.'

'But you're not supposed to have them cut off till next month,' said Pinkity, longing to snip them off.

'Never mind! Cut them off *now!* Oh do, Pinkity, dear, dear Pinkity,' begged the lambs.

'All right, I'd love to!' answered the naughty little pixie. 'Come here, Long-

legs, I'll do you first!'

Little Long-legs frisked up, and snip! snip! went the big scissors.

'There,' said Pinkity, 'I've cut your tail off. Do you feel cooler?'

'Oh yes, yes,' said the lamb, skipping away in delight. 'That's *much* better!'

'Come along, Frisky, let me do yours,' laughed Pinkity, waving his big scissors.

One by one each of the little lambs came up to Pinkity, and had its long, heavy tail cut off. Soon the grass was covered with little tails, and Pinkity's arm began to ache.

'There!' he said, as he cut off the very last one. 'There! That's all! Now I'll give Togs the Tailor his scissors.'

Pinkity flew off and put the big

scissors down by Togs the Tailor, who was still asleep, and then made friends with two bumble bees, who gave him a good feast of honey for his dinner.

Soon he heard a great noise, and flew into the fields to see what it was.

He saw the Lord High Chancellor of Fairy-land in the fields shaking Togs the Tailor angrily and scolding him.

'What do you mean by cutting off the lambs' tails? he roared. 'Don't you know they are never cut until next month? How dare you?'

'I didn't, your Highness, I didn't!' said poor old Togs, the tears running down his cheeks. 'I wouldn't do such a thing, really and truly I wouldn't!'

Pinkity felt very much upset. He knew he had done something naughty, and he wasn't very sorry about it; but he couldn't bear to see poor old Togs punished for something he hadn't done.

He flew straight down into the field, and knelt before the astonished Lord Chancellor.

'Please, your Highness,' he cried, 'don't punish Togs. *I* took his scissors whilst he was asleep, and cut the lambs' tails off.'

The Chancellor let Togs go and stared at Pinkity.

'Oho!' he said. 'You're the pixie who poured water on us this morning! Come here and be whipped!'

He whipped Pinkity hard, and then looked at him.

'Although you're naughty,' he said, 'I am pleased that you came and owned up when I was scolding Togs for something *you had* done. I shan't punish you for cutting off the lambs' tails, but I shall see that you always have work to do now, instead of flying

14

about all day and playing tricks.'

'Let him clear up all these lambs' tails,' said Togs the Tailor.

'Yes, I will. Go and hang them on the hazel-nut trees, Pinkity. They want cheering up a bit. And mind, if you play any more tricks, I'll whip you again! Now, off you go!'

Off went naughty little Pinkity, carrying an armful of lambs' tails. He hung

15

them on the hazel-nut twigs, and very pretty they looked too, all shaking in the wind.

Pinkity is still sometimes naughty, but he's so busy, especially in spring-time, that he doesn't find time for *many* tricks.

And if you look on the hazel trees you will find the little lambs' tails hanging there, and if your eyes are extra sharp,

you *might* see Pinkity flying from twig to twig, watching them shake and wiggle in the wind, just as they did when they grew on the little fairy lambs!

16

2

The Careless Hedgehogs

Once upon a time, Hoo, the white owl, found a baby elf cuddled up in his nest.

'Tu-whit!' he said, most astonished. 'Who are you?'

The baby elf stared at him, but didn't answer a word.

Hoo perched on the side of his nest, and wondered what he should do with the strange little creature.

'I'll go and ask my friend Prickles,' he said at last. 'He is wise, and will tell me.'

Off he flew.

Prickles, the hedgehog, was awake, just outside his house.

'Good evening,' said Hoo politely.

'Good evening,' answered Prickles. 'why have you come to see me?'

'In my nest there is a strange little elf

thing, that will not speak a word,' explained Hoo. 'What I am to do with it?'

'A little elf thing!' said Prickles, sitting up quickly. 'What is it like?'

'It is small, with yellow wings,' answered Hoo.

'Have you seen the notice the King of Fairyland has put up everywhere?' asked Prickles excitedly.

'No,' said Hoo.

'Come and I'll show it to you,' said Prickles, scuttling off.

Presently they came to a tall foxglove. Hanging upon it was a notice which said, –

LOST FROM DREAMLAND
A LITTLE ELF BABY WITH YELLOW
WINGS. ANYONE FINDING IT SHALL
HAVE A GREAT REWARD
PLEASE TELL THE

KING OF FAIRYLAND

'There!' said Prickles. 'You must have found the lost baby elf.'

'But how could it have got into my

19

nest?' asked Hoo, very puzzled.

'Don't bother about *that!*' answered Prickles. 'Go and tell the King you've found it!'

'Will you take care of it while I'm gone?' asked Hoo.

'Yes,' said Prickles. 'I'll get all the fairy hedgehogs I know to look after it.'

'So Hoo flew down to the hedgehogs, carrying the elf baby gently.

'Now look after it carefully,' he said, flying off to the King's palace.

All the fairy hedgehogs sat down in a ring, and looked at the baby. It lay in the middle of them and laughed and kicked.

'I think perhaps the bad gnomes stole it,' said Prickles. 'They are enemies to the people of Dreamland.'

20

Whenever any one came near the little baby, the hedgehogs stiffened all their prickles, and made the very worst noise they could.

'Here comes Hoo!' cried Prickles at last. Hoo perched on the tree above him.

'It *is* the lost baby,' he cried, 'and the King of Dreamland is coming to fetch it in two days. Our King says you must take great care of it till then, and give it honey to eat and dew to drink.'

21

'Very well,' said Prickles.

'And,' said Hoo flying off, 'you must see that the bad gnomes don't come for it again.'

So all that day the hedgehogs watched the elf baby. Prickles fetched it honey from the heather and dew from the grasses. All through the night the fairy hedgehogs watched, and next day Prickes said, –

'I'm going to fetch a special dew from

the red blackberry leaves. Be very careful while I am gone.'

Off he went.

Then one of the little hedgehogs stretched itself.

'I'm *so* tired of watching,' he said, 'I'm going off for a little walk.'

He ran off through the grass, but in a minute he came back looking very excited.

'Come quickly!' he cried, 'there is a fairy dance by the foxgloves tonight, and if we're quick we can all go and hear the music.'

The hedgehogs thought that would be lovely.

'We'll go to the dance till Prickles comes back!' they cried, 'he'll never know.'

Off they scampered as hard as they could, and were soon having a glorious time.

The little elf baby, finding there was nobody to stop it crawled away by itself, and fell fast asleep under a mushroom a little way off.

Suddenly there was a great fluttering of wings, and down flew the King of Dreamland and the King of Fairyland;

they had come to fetch the lost elf baby. At the same moment up came Prickles too, with his blackberry dew for the baby.

'Where is the baby?' cried the King of Dreamland.

'I don't know,' answered Prickles, looking astonished. 'It was here when I left, guarded by lots of fairy hedgehogs. Now they're all gone!'

At that moment, back came the hedgehogs from the dance. They looked very frightened when they saw that the baby was gone and the two Kings had come.

'How *dare* you disobey my orders?' said the King of Fairyland to the trembling hedgehogs. 'Now the baby has gone again, and perhaps the bad gnomes have stolen it away just because you weren't watching!'

'Please, we're very sorry,' said the hedgehogs.

'That doesn't help matters,' said the Dreamland King angrily.

'I shall have to punish you,' said the

Fairy King, 'You haven't been good hedgehogs, so perhaps you will be good if I change you into something else!'

He waved his hand. In a minute all the fairy hedgehogs found themselves climbing up a big chestnut tree.

The King waved his wand again.

The hedgehogs climbed along the branches, turned green, and sat quite still.

'There!' said the King. 'Now perhaps they will keep the baby chestnuts from harm until they're ripe. Now, Prickles,

hunt around until you find the elf baby.'

Of course Prickles found him under the mushroom very quickly, and brought him back to the King of Dreamland.

But Prickles is very lonely now without the other hedgehogs. They never come down to play with him, because they are so busy looking after the baby chestnuts, and they are much more careful of them than they were of the little elf baby.

And if you look at a chestnut tree in October, you'll see what the King changed the hedgehogs into – and you'll find they're still very prickly!

3

The Three Naughty Gnomes

Once upon a time there lived a little family of gnomes in Fairyland, and they all worked hard every day.

They made little pipes for the baby fairies to blow bubbles with. They made them most beautifully too, and the babies loved them.

Ding made the pipes, Dong carved little patterns round the bowls of the pipes, and Dell blew bubbles with them, just to see if they worked all right.

'How lovely!' cried the baby fairies, sitting in a ring round the three gnomes. 'Do let us have some to play with.'

'Here's one for you, Briony, and one for you, Melilot,' said Dell, giving out the little carved pipes.

The babies dipped their pipes into the

frothy soap and blew hard. They blew
the most glorious bubbles, blue and
mauve, green and orange. Off they
floated away in the air, and the South
Wind had a great game chasing them.

One day when Ding, Dong, and Dell
sat making their pipes, Hoo, the big
grey owl, flew silently down to them.

'Good afternoon,' said the little gnomes
politely.

'Good afternoon,' answered Hoo. 'What
are you making?'

30

'We are making pipes for the baby fairies to blow bubbles with,' said Ding, giving Hoo one to look at.

'How do you blow bubbles?' asked the grey owl.

'Like this!' said Dell, dipping a carved pipe into the water and blowing an immense bubble into Hoo's face. It touched his sharp beak and burst!

'Goodness gracious me!' exclaimed Hoo, very startled. 'Wherever has it gone to?'

Ding, Dong and Dell laughed till they couldn't laugh any more!

But Hoo didn't like being laughed at.

'Your pipes are silly pipes,' he said. 'They only blow things that burst themselves away. Now *I* could tell you of some wonderful pipes I've seen in the world of boys and girls.'

'Tell us!' begged all the little gnomes.

'These pipes,' went on Hoo, 'are filled with dried leaves of some strange plant, and when they are touched with fire, blue smoke comes from the bowls of the pipes, and a curious smell.'

'Pipes that smoke!' cried the three gnomes. 'How wonderful! Ours can only blow bubbles.'

32

'Tu-whit, tu-whit!' called Hoo, flying off into the trees. 'Why don't you make *your* pipes smoke? That would be funnier then bursting bubbles on my nose.'

'*Shall* we make ours smoke?' asked Ding, thinking it would be a great idea.

'Do you think we ought to?' said Dong. 'The Fairy Queen said they were only to be used for fairy bubbles, you know.'

'Oh, *do* let's!' cried Dell. 'Perhaps the Queen didn't know about making pipes smoke.'

'She knows everything,' said Dong. 'Hadn't we better ask her first before we do?'

'Oh no!' said Ding, 'because then she might say no. Let's ask her afterwards.'

That was what the naughty little gnomes decided to do.

'We can't get the dried leaves that are smoked in the land of boys and girls,' said Dell, 'so we'll dry some rose leaves instead, and smoke those.'

So all the next day Ding, Dong and

Dell collected wild rose leaves and dried them in the sun. The baby fairies were tremendously excited about it all and were longing to see what was going to happen.

'Hurry up!' they cried, 'we want to see the smoke coming from our bubble pipes!'

That evening, when all the rose leaves were ready, the three gnomes filled three little pipes and put them in their mouths.

'Now, we must have fire,' they said. 'Let us call the fireflies and ask them to help us.'

The fireflies came dancing up and

darted in and out of the pipes. As their little gleaming bodies touched the dried rose leaves, they set them alight and there were the three gnomes smoking pipes just as Daddies do in the world of boys and girls!

'Oh how lovely,' cried the fairies, clapping their hands. 'Give us some pipes, and let us do the same, Dell! What a lovely smell!'

'No, *you* mustn't,' answered Dell. 'The Queen wouldn't like it.'

'We shall, so there!' cried the naughty babies, snatching up some pipes. They quickly filled them with rose leaves, called the fireflies, and soon they were all smoking too!

The air grew thick with rose-leaf smoke, and the South Wind blew it away. It passed where the Fairy Queen was sitting looking at the new moon, and she was most astonished.

'Whatever is that?' she cried, and got up quickly. 'Who can be burning rose leaves in Fairyland?'

'The South Wind told her who it was, and she hurried away to the home of Ding, Dong, and Dell.

'You naughty children!' she cried, as she saw the fairies with their pipes filled with rose leaves. 'Put down your pipes at once!'

The fairies put them down, feeling rather frightened.

'Do you know what happens when people smoke when they are little?' asked the queen sternly.

'No, your Majesty,' answered the babies.

'Well, they feel *dreadfully* ill,' said the Queen, 'and that's just what *you'll* do. Go home to bed, all of you, and when you begin feeling ill, just remember it's a punishment to you for doing something you knew you shouldn't.'

All the babies flew off, looking very miserable.

'As for you,' went on the Queen, turning to Ding, Dong and Dell, 'you are too old to feel ill because you smoked. But I cannot trust you any more to make pipes for my baby fairies. You must use them for something else.'

'But we *can't*, your Majesty,' said Ding, beginning to cry. 'They're just pipes for blowing bubbles!'

'Oh yes, you can,' answered the Queen. 'Go to the oak trees, and put all the acorns you can see in the bowls of your pipes. The handle of the pipe will do for a stalk to hold it to the tree. Those acorns are always tumbling off before they are ripe.'

'Yes, your Majesty,' said the little gnomes.

'Now put them in properly,' said the Queen, 'and mind you find acorns to fit. I'll forgive you when I see you are really working well.'

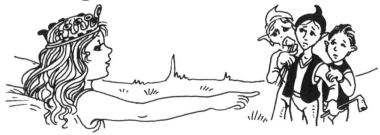

The gnomes flew off to the oak trees. And next time *you* come to an oak tree, you can see how nicely Dong has carved all the acorn-cups, and how beautifully Ding and Dell have fitted shiny acorns into all their little fairy pipes!

4

Sativus and the Pots of Gold

Long years ago there lived a little gnome called Sativus. He lived all by himself and the fairies knew very little of him.

'He is very poor and quite harmless,' they told the Queen when she asked them about him.

But the fairies were quite wrong when they said Sativus was poor. He wasn't. He was very rich indeed. He had pots and pots of bright yellow gold hidden away in a secret cupboard.

'Ha! ha!' chuckled Sativus, as he opened the door and looked at it. 'Tonight I will add some more to my store of gold!'

He put on his red cloak and crept

away into the shadows outside. He went to an elm tree, climbed into its hollow trunk, and disappeared down some steps.

Down and down he went till he came to a long passage which led upwards for a long way.

'Here I am at last!' said Sativus in a pleased voice, as he came out into the open again on the top of a hill.

This hill was Rainbow Hill, which one end of the rainbow touched when the rain fairies hung it in the sky.

41

Sativus had discovered it quite by chance, and had been astonished to find a pot of yellow gold on the top of the hill.

Who had put it there he had no idea, but as it seemed to belong to nobody, he took it home.

He had visited Rainbow Hill many times afterwards, and each time carried away a pot of gold, though sometimes he had been forced to dig a long time before discovering it.

'I hope I'll find a pot quickly,' said Sativus to himself, as he dug into the grass.

'Hurray!' he cried a minute later; 'I'm lucky tonight – here's a pot of gold already! and what a big one!'

Sativus tugged at the pot until he had

pulled it from the earth. It was full to the brim with large round yellow pieces of gold!

Back went the little gnome to his house, and put it with the others. Then, carefully shutting the windows and pulling down the blinds, he started to count all the gold pieces he had.

Presently there came a knock at the door.

'Sativus! Sativus! We're going to have a dance tonight. Come and join us!' called a voice.

43

Sativus clutched his gold. 'No, no! I can't!' he answered. 'I'm too busy!'

'Oh, what a pity,' said the voice, disappointed. 'Good-bye!'

Some time later there came another knock at the door.

'Sativus! Lend me your cloak! I've come without mine, and I'm cold!' begged another voice.

'I can't lend you mine, it has too many holes in it,' answered Sativus crossly.

Now this wasn't true. His cloak was perfectly good, but Sativus simply

didn't want the bother of getting it, he wanted to go on playing with his gold.

Night after night this happened, until the fairies left the little gnome quite alone, and he was happy.

Now, one rainy, windy night, there came a knock at his door.

'Sativus, friend Sativus! - let me in!' pleaded a little voice. 'I am your friend Bron, and I am cold and hungry.'

Sativus frowned. He had just spread his gold out on the table, and was going to have a lovely time alone with it.

'I am busy, friend Bron,' he replied.
'Can you not go to Meril's – he lives near
by.'

'I've hurt my ankle,' said Bron. 'I
would rather spend the night with you.'

Sativus made no answer. He thought
perhaps if Bron heard nothing further,
he would go on to Meril's. And, after a
while, he heard Bron's footsteps going
down the path.

'Now I can enjoy myself,' chuckled
Sativus, taking up his gold.

Next morning Sativus was surprised
to see something lying by his gate. It
was Bron, who had been unable to walk

any farther, and had lain there in the wind and rain all night.

'Oh, Bron, Bron!' sobbed Sativus, lifting up his friend, and carrying him indoors. 'How could I have been so unkind! It was all because of my gold!

Oh, if only you get better I'll throw it all away!'

He nursed his friend day after day, and when at last the time came that Bron was able to walk, Sativus took all his beloved pots of gold and journeyed to the Fairy Queen.

'You have done great wrong,' said the Queen gently, when she heard his tale. 'But if you are truly sorry, something good may come of your gold yet.'

'Please your Majesty, won't *you* have it?' asked Sativus.

'No, I don't need gold,' said the Queen. 'Do as you decided to do, and throw it away, Sativus. Stand on top of the Rainbow Hill and throw it as far as you can, and see what happens.'

So Savitus went to Rainbow Hill, and standing there, he took his gold pieces one by one, and threw them far and wide over the world.

'Come back next springtime, Sativus!' said the Queen, 'and we will see if anything good has come.'

So the next springtime Sativus and the Queen stood on Rainbow Hill, and looked far and wide.

'Your Majesty' shouted Sativus, 'see – my gold has made the world beautiful!'

And it had – for all over the countryside grew little gold flowers – deep yellow as the gold pieces themselves.

'I told you some good would come!' said the Queen. 'You have given the world a beautiful gift!'

And if you look in your gardens early in the year, you will see what Sativus has given you – a lovely deep yellow crocus!

5

The Naughty Smoke Fairies

Once upon a time a crowd of tiny little smoke fairies escaped from a bonfire. No one saw them go, and they took good care not to be seen as they slipped away into the open fields.

'Hurray!' said one, turning head over heels, 'now we're free of that nasty old fire!'

'Yes, and we've got no work to do,' shouted another, swinging on a big daisy, and leaving little black marks on its white petals. They were dreadfully black little fairies, as black as soot, for, of course, they had lived in smoke all their lives, because their duty was to take the horrid black smoke away from where children breathe, right up into the air among the clouds.

'Let's have some fun, and be really naughty,' said a third little fairy. 'I'm so tired of always being good and doing my work properly.'

'Yes, let's!' said all the others.

Presently the smoke fairies came to a large ring where toadstools grew. There they found fairy carpenters busy at work putting the toadstools in a ring so that the fairies might dance inside, and sit on the toadstools for supper.

'Oh, just look,' whispered one of the smoke fairies, pointing to an oak tree. The others looked. The oak tree had, at the bottom by the roots, a little door leading into a cupboad. In this cupboard were stored all the lovely things for the party, cakes and sweets, jellies and honey-dew drinks.

'Do you think we might come to the party?' the smoke fairies asked the carpenters.

'Not if you haven't been invited,' answered the busy workers.

'We haven't been asked,' said a smoke fairy sadly.

'You are very naughty to be here then,' said carpenter severely. 'If you haven't got a holiday for the party, then you should be at work.'

'Oh, bother!' cried the smoke fairies crossly, 'we *shan't* go back to work and

we'll be as naughty as we can, so there!'

'Well, good-bye,' said the carpenters, flying off. 'We're going to get ready for the party.'

The smoke fairies sat down and frowned. 'Let's do something very, *very* bad,' said one. 'It's not fair that we haven't been asked.'

'I know!' exlaimed a tiny little black fairy; 'Let's saw the toadstools half-way through, so that when the fairies sit on them tonight, they'll all break, and tumble them off!'

'Oh yes, what fun!' said the naughty little fairies. They picked up some of the saws that the carpenters had left, and soon had all the toadstools sawn half-way through.

'I'm so hungry,' sighed the biggest fairy.

'Let's have a jelly out of the oak tree cupboard!' suggested another.

They all peeped into the cupboard, and chose something to eat. And what do you think – they were so dreadfully hungry that, in about ten minutes, they had eaten *every single thing* in that cupboard!

Then they all flew up into the trees, to watch the fairy dance. One by one all the fairy guests arrived, and presently the King and Queen arrived too. Then the dancing began, and merrily the little fairies stepped in the fairy ring.

When the signal was given for supper, the smoke fairies began to feel uncomfortable, for 'Oh dear!' cried a little fairy, tumbling off a broken toadstool!

'Oh dear!' cried another.

'Oh dear!' cried a third.

One by one all the toadstools broke, and the astonished little fairies found themselves on the grass.

The King stood up, looking angry to think that such a trick had been played on the fairies.

Just then some little red fairies cried out, 'Your Majesty! the cupboard is empty, and there is nothing to eat!'

'Who has done these naughty things?' thundered the King.

There was no answer, but the smoke fairies began to feel very afraid up in the tree.

'If you please,' said a blue and white fairy, 'I believe it's some smoke fairies who have escaped from their work.'

'Oh, there they are, there they are!' shouted a yellow fairy, pointing up into the oak tree.

The smoke fairies, now thoroughly frightened, flew off as fast as they could, with all the others after them. They came to a field where there were a lot of red poppies. Very quickly each smoke fairy crept inside a poppy and closed the red petals round, and waited there hidden.

But alas! the King and Queen soon found them, and made them come out.

'Now, tell me why you have been so naughty,' said the King.

'Please, your Majesty,' said the biggest smoke fairy, 'it's because we were tired of our work, and we wanted to come to the party, and couldn't.'

'That is your own fault,' said the King. 'I sent you all an invitation, but my messenger found you had run away from your work, and so he couldn't give it to you.'

The smoke fairies began to cry.

'Oh, we *are* so sorry we've spoilt your party too! Please forgive us, and we'll go back to our work!'

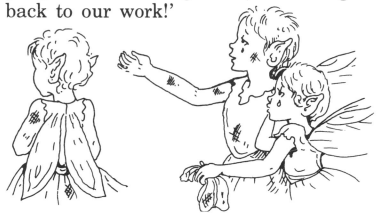

'I'll forgive you,' answered the King kindly; 'and I will give you some other work to do if you are tired of carrying the smoke up into the air. You shall polish the black beetles for me every morning, and sleep in the poppies at night.'

'Oh, thank you, thank you,' cried the little smoke fairies, jumping back into their poppies.

'Good-bye,' said the King, and back they all went to finish the dance.

So those little smoke fairies live in the poppies now, and if you look into the middle of one, perhaps you can guess why it is so *very* black, and why, when you touch it, black, sooty powder comes off on your fingers!

6

The Rose that didn't Grow

Once upon a time the King of Fairyland had a wonderful rose garden.

As he walked through it one day, examining all the buds and smelling all the full-blown roses, he sighed.

'We have plenty of red roses and plenty of pink and white,' he said to the Head Gardener, 'and I know them all, every one. Don't you think it's about time we had some new kinds?'

'Your Majesty,' answered the Head Gardener, 'you already have all the kinds there are. There are no new roses to be had in all Fairyland.'

'Well, that's ridiculous,' said the King. 'Why, in the world of boys and girls people are *always* inventing new roses. Why can't *we* invent some new sorts?

I'd like a yellow rose. We've red and white, pink and cream, but not a single yellow one!'

'Well, your Majesty,' suggested the Gardener, 'why don't you send out a Royal Proclamation, asking every one to set their wits to work and grow some new kinds of roses? It's just the sort of

thing the elves and fairies love to do!'

'Good! Splendid idea!' cried the King. 'I'll go and do it at once!' and away he hurried into the palace, and called for pen and ink and paper.

Then, because he was an excellent writer, the King wrote out the Proclamation himself. When it was finished he blotted it carefully and gave it to the Lord High Chamberlain.

'Make this Proclamation known throughout the kingdom,' he ordered.

'Yes, your Majesty,' answered the Chamberlain, and hurried off.

In a little while all the heralds of Fairyland were blowing their trumpets, and calling out the King's Proclamation to crowds of excited fairies.

'Oyez, oyez, oyez!' they called, in their clear, silvery voices. 'The King of Fairyland offers a reward to whomso-

ever will bring him the most beautiful new yellow rose. The winner will be made Grand Keeper of all the Flowers. Oyez, oyez, oyez!'

Then began such an excitement in Fairyland! Pixies and elves, gnomes and fairies hurried to their gardens to see if they could, by help of what magic they knew, change the roses growing there into beautiful yellow ones.

'I'm going to look up spells in an old book of magic I've got!' said one, turning out a cupboard to find it. She turned over page after page of the book until she came to the word YELLOW.

'To make anything change its colour to yellow, dance lightly on one foot four times round the object, morning and evening, chanting the magic word "Fala-gari-oona-ree!" cried the fairy, reading from the book.

So morning and evening the fairy could be seen lightly dancing on one foot and singing to the big red rose tree in her garden. Day by day it changed its colour little by little, and the fairy was most excited.

A little elf had a great idea. 'If I water my rose tree with something yellow, that will turn the flowers yellow! he thought, and he hunted about for something golden.

At last he made a mixture of early morning sunshine and amber yellow dewdrops, and every day he watered his rose tree with them, until the rosebuds began to look as yellow as the sunbeams.

The pixies, who had a splendid rose garden of their own, met together to consult as to what plan *they* follow.

'I know,' cried one. 'Let's mix a strong and powerful yellow paint, and get Artis, who paints exquisitely, to colour all our white roses yellow for us! If the king says a magic spell over them the colour will stay on always, and next year's flowers will be yellow too!'

'Spendid!' cried the rest. 'Now, let's all go and find something to make the paint.' Off they went, into all the corners of Fairyland.

One scooped the yellow sunshine from the tops of pools at sunrise.

Another begged the brimstone butterfly for some of the yellow dust on his wings. And a third had a spendid idea. *He* went about with a long silver spoon, and took the gold that lies in the heart of daffodils.

Many other pixies brought yellow powders and yellow dust for the paint, and when they were all ready, they were shaken into a glass jar, and stirred up with the frosted cobwebs to make them sticky. The yellow fairy paint gleamed through the glass, a glorious colour that glistened and shone curiously.

'Artis! Artis!' called the excited pixies. 'Come here quickly, and look!'

Artis came forward slowly. He was a queer little dreamy fairy, with big ears and deep brown eyes that saw many things no other fairy could see. He carried a big palette and many brushes.

'What a beautiful colour! he cried in astonishment as he saw the glass jar. 'Oh! give me some to use for my painting!'

'Yes, we will, if you'll do something for us!' said the pixies. 'See, we want you to paint our white roses yellow for us. Will you?'

'Of course I will,' promised Artis, picking up the jar. 'I'll begin at once. I'd *love* to do that!' and off he hurried into the pixie rose garden. He settled himself down by the wall, in the shade, and carefully began to paint a large rosebud.

Now, over the wall, in a little

higgledy-piggledy house, lived a tiny gnome. His name was Acaulis, and he was very excited when he heard that the King wanted a yellow rose.

'I'll look at the rose tree in my garden,' he said to himself, and hurried home to see.

But alas! his rose tree was dead!

'Oh dear! oh dear!' sighed Acaulis;

now what shall I do! I *must* take a yellow rose to the King somehow or other!'

He sat and thought for a long time – and then, he had many a time done a good turn to the Simple Witch, who lived away in the hills, he decided to go and ask her help.

When he arrived at her cottage she

was busy undoing a purple packet.

'Good morning,' she said. 'I know what you want, so don't bother to tell me. I'll help you if I can.'

72

'Good morning, and thank you,' answered Acaulis politely, quite used to the queer ways of the witch.

'Now, look,' said the Simple Witch suddenly. 'Here are some yellow seeds from the land of Makebelieve. I am going to give you one, Acaulis, for you have often been kind to me. If you follow all my directions carefully you will have a beautiful yellow rose, far more beautiful in colour, shape, and smell than any other.'

'You are very kind indeed,' said Acaulis gratefully. 'Tell me what I must do.'

The Simple Witch threw one of the yellow seeds into a pot over the fire, and stirred it about, while she chanted a magic song.

"Sweet and mellow,
Rich and yellow;
Even so
May you grow,"

sang the Witch. Then she picked out the seed again and gave it to Acaulis.

73

'Plant it,' she said. 'Water it with honey and dew on each Friday evening just before sunset. If you miss watering it, it will not grow properly. Good-bye.'

'Good-bye,' said Acaulis gratefully, and ran off as fast as he could to plant the magic seed.

He planted it, and then went to buy a pot of honey from the Bee-Woman, so that when Friday came he could water it with dew and honey.

One day he heard Artis singing, and he popped his head over the wall of the Pixie rose garden.

'Hullo, Artis!' he called. 'What are you doing?'

'Painting white roses yellow!' answered Artis. 'See what a lot I've done!'

'How beautiful they are!' marvelled Acaulis. 'You do paint spendidly, Artis!'

After that the little gnome sat on the wall every day and talked to Artis. The two soon became very fond of one

another, for both were merry, sunny little creatures.

On the first Friday evening Acaulis mixed dew and honey together and carefully watered the tiny little plant growing from his seed. 'I *do* hope it will be beautiful,' said Acaulis to himself, 'for I would so love to be Grand Keeper of the Flowers!'

On the second Friday evening, just as Acaulis was preparing the dew and honey, there came a knock at his door.

'Acaulis, Acaulis! Come quickly! Misty-May has caught her wing in a bramble, and she wants you to get it free for her!' cried a voice.

'Oh, I *can't* come!' answered Acaulis. 'I *must* water my rose plant!'

'*Do* come! *do* come!' begged the voice.

Kind-hearted Acaulis put down the honey-pot and ran out to the woods to help Misty-May.

But alas! when he returned the sun had set, and it was too late to water his plant!

'Oh, now it won't grow, it won't grow!' wept Acaulis. then he dried his eyes. 'Never mind. Perhaps if I give it *two* lots of honey and dew next Friday it won't matter,' he decided.

All that week the plant did not grow a single inch, and Acaulis was very upset. On the next Friday, as he was hurrying home to water his plant, he met his friend Grey-Ears, the rabbit, carrying a

load of green moon-beads to the Queen's
dressmaker.

'We're going the same way, Grey-
Ears,' said Acaulis. 'Let me carry your
load for you for a little while.'

'Thank you very much,' said Grey-
Ears, and gave the moon-beads to
Acaulis.

They hurried along till suddenly
Acaulis tripped over a tree stump and –
clitter-clatter, clitter-clatter! All the green
moon-beads rolled here, there, and
everywhere.

'Oh, they'll be lost! Whatever shall I

do!' cried Grey-Ears in despair.

'I'm *dreadfully* sorry!' said poor little Acaulis. 'I'll pick them all up for you, really I will.'

And he did. But by the time he had

hunted under all the leaves and in all the moss the sun had set, and another Friday evening had gone by without his precious plant being watered. Acaulis was dreadfully upset.

'I'll stay home next Friday and make sure it is watered,' he said to himself.

So the next Friday he stayed at home. Just as he was getting down the little honey-pot a pixie rushed in.

'Artis is ill! He has a terrible sore throat and he's got to eat pots and pots of honey to make him better. Have you got any to spare?'

'Oh dear! I *did* so want it; but never mind, take my honey for Artis,' said Acaulis, with tears in his eyes, giving the precious pot of honey to the pixie. The pixie ran off, and Acaulis went out and watered his tiny plant with dew alone, though he knew that wouldn't do any good at all. But there wasn't enough time before sunset to get any more honey from the Bee-Woman.

The plant didn't grow at all. It had a funny little collection of leaves growing all together, and a few yellowish buds. Acaulis thought it was rather pretty, but a very poor specimen for a rose.

'Anyway, I'll take it to the King,' he decided. 'He might happen to like it.'

On the evening before the Rose Show a great rain-storm came. Acaulis peeped over the wall, and saw, to his dismay, that the drenching rain was washing all the colour off the roses that Artis had painted so carefully. He hurriedly climbed over the wall, took off his cap, and held it over one really beautiful yellow rose that the rain had hardly spoilt.

'This will save *one* of Artis's roses, anyhow,' said Acaulis, and stayed there till the rain had stopped, and the pixies came running out.

'Oh you *are* a good friend!' they cried to Acaulis. 'Artis will be so pleased to have one left. He was afraid they would all be spoilt for tomorrow. He couldn't come out because his throat isn't better; but he's going to the Rose Show tomorrow!'

Acaulis ran back to his cottage and dried himself. He felt quite sure Artis's rose would win the prize, and though he would have liked to be the Grand Keeper of the Flowers himself, he felt there was no hope now, for his plant was so small and queer.

Next day pixies, elves, gnomes, and fairies crowded to the palace, bringing their pots and bowls of roses, each hoping to win the prize. They arranged them all in a row, and stood by them, waiting for the King.

'Oh, oh! Just look at Acaulis's plant!' laughed the fairies, pointing to it.

'Poor little plant!' said Acaulis. 'You might have grown beautifully if only I'd been able to water you. Never mind, I'll make you look ever so sweet and tidy, and perhaps the King will smile at you!'

So Acaulis arranged the leaves in a rosette around the buds, and bunched the buds together in the middle. One or two were out, and were a beautiful pale yellow, but very small and with only five petals.

Soon the King came along. He looked at the rose of the fairy who had danced round her bush morning and night.

'It is beautiful,' he said; 'but you have danced too much, and the rose is orange, not yellow.'

Then he looked at the rose of the elf who had watered his with sunshine and amber dewdrops.

'You have a beautiful rose,' he said; 'but see, your watering has turned the leaves and the stem yellow too, and that is ugly.'

He looked at many others, but not one did he find that was perfect, until he came to the one that Artis had painted.

'Oh, how glorious!' he said. 'This is the one I shall choose.'

'Please, your Majesty, it is painted,' said Artis. 'Will you say a magic spell over it, to make the paint stay always? And look, you haven't seen my friend's rose yet,' and he pointed to where Acaulis stood.

'What a queer, prim little rose!' said the King, looking at the tidy little plant. 'It isn't a *bit* like a rose, Acaulis, but it's a lovely yellow. Does it smell?'

'Yes, your Majesty,' said Acaulis.

The King smelt it.

'Oh, Acaulis, it smells of the springtime,' cried the King excitedly. 'No flower has ever had such an exquisite, faint spring smell before! How *did* you grow such a flower?'

'Let *me* tell you, your Majesty,' said Artis.' And he not only told the King about the flower, but about all the kind deeds Acaulis had done instead of tending his plant as he wanted to.

'You are a good little gnome, Acaulis,' said the King gently. 'I cannot give you the prize, because that must go to Artis; but because your flower is so dainty and smells of springtime, it shall be planted all over the country, to come out in the very early spring, and every one will love it.

Acaulis was tremendously pleased.

'What shall we call my flower?' he asked.

The King laughed. 'It's such a funny little prim and proper flower!' he said. 'Let's call it a primrose, shall we?'

And we still call the little yellow flower of the springtime the primrose, and if you are very sharp one day, you *might* see Acaulis arranging the leaves in a rosette, and enjoying the smell of springtime in the pale yellow blossoms of his precious flowers.

7

A Basket of Surprises

When Jimmy's mother went to the Garden Fair at the Vicarage she bought a very beautiful basket. It was large and round and deep, and had a fine, strong handle. All round the basket was a pretty green and yellow pattern. It really was a very fine basket, and Jimmy's mother was pleased with it.

'Now, you are not to borrow this basket for anything, Jimmy,' she said to him. 'You can have my old one if you want one. This is to be kept for special things, like taking eggs to Granny, or something like that.'

Jimmy promised. He was once allowed to take some flowers in the basket to old Mr. White, but that was all. And then one day he wanted a basket to take his trains, signals and lines to his friend's, Billy Brown. He went to find the old basket and it wasn't there. His mother was out and no one was at home except Tibby, the big tabby cat, sitting by the fire.

'Where's the old basket, Tibby?' Jimmy asked her. But she just mewed and sat on by the fire, thinking her

pussy thoughts. Jimmy hunted everywhere. There was no old basket to be found at all. Perhaps his mother had taken it.

'Well, I'll have to take the new basket,' said Jimmy. 'I can't possibly take all my things without a basket.'

So he took down the beautiful new basket and packed his things into it.

88

Then off he went to Billy's and had a nice tea and a nice game. Billy begged him to lend him his railway for a day, so Jimmy said he would. He set off home with the empty basket, swinging it by the big handle.

He had to go through the woods on his way home, and as he ran he saw a bird fly into a bush. 'Hallo!' thought Jimmy, 'There's a nest there. I'll just peep and see. I won't disturb the bird in case it deserts its nest – but I would just like to see if there are any baby birds there.'

He pushed his way into the bush, but the bird flew out again and into another

89

bush. Jimmy followed her. He felt sure
she must have a nest somewhere. But
she hadn't. She was just looking for the
caterpillars there.

Jimmy set off home again – but
suddenly he remembered that he had
put down his basket somewhere. Goodness! Where could it be?

He ran back – but no matter how he
looked he couldn't find that basket
anywhere! 'Oh, dear!' thought Jimmy,
as he hunted. 'Whatever will Mummy
say if I go home without it? I am sure I
put it down by the bush I first looked in.'

But Jimmy couldn't find the bush!

And at last he had to go home without the basket. When he told his mother he had lost it she was very cross.

'You are a naughty boy, Jimmy,' she said. 'I told you not to borrow my best basket. Now, unless it is found again, you must save up your money and buy me a new one.'

'Oh, but Mummy, I'm saving up to buy a railway tunnel!' cried Jimmy, in dismay.

'Well, I'm sorry, dear, but you can't buy your tunnel until you have bought a new basket,' said his mother. 'You had better go and have another hunt for it.'

Poor Jimmy! He went and hunted and

hunted, but he could not find that basket! The next day his Uncle Peter came to see him and gave him a whole twenty pence to spend – but his mother said he was to put it into his money-box to save up for the new basket. He was dreadfully disappointed. The next morning his mother called him and said: 'Have ·you seen Tibby, Jimmy? She isn't in her usual place by the fire, and she hasn't been in for her break-fast.'

'No, I haven't seen her,' said Jimmy quite worried, for he was very fond of Tibby. 'Where can she be?'

'Perhaps she will come in for her dinner,' said his mother. But Tibby didn't. There was no sign of her at all. Jimmy got more and more worried. He had had Tibby from a kitten, and the two were great friends. He did so hope she hadn't got caught in a trap.

'Do you think she has, Mummy?' he asked. 'Oh, wouldn't it be dreadful if she had gone rabbiting in the woods and got caught in a trap and nobody was

there to set her free?'

'Oh, I don't expect she has, for a moment,' said his mother. 'She hardly ever goes rabbiting. She will turn up, I expect. Now, what are you going to do this afternoon, Jimmy? You said you wanted to go and play with Billy Brown.'

'Well, I did want to,' said Jimmy. 'But I think I'll just go and hunt for Tibby, Mummy. I do feel unhappy about her, really I do.'

'After tea we will catch the bus and go into the town to buy a new basket,' said his mother. 'I really must have another. I think you have enough money in your box now to buy me one.'

Jimmy went off to hunt for Tibby, feeling very miserable. 'I've lost Tibby, and I've got to give up my railway tunnel and buy a new basket instead,' he sighed, as he ran along to the woods. 'What a lot of bad luck all at once!'

He soon came to the woods, and he began hunting about, calling Tibby. He felt sure she must have been caught in a trap.

'Tibby, Tibby, Tibby!' he cried. 'Where are you? Tibby, Tibby, Tibby!'

For some time he could hear nothing but the wind in the trees and the singing of the birds. Then he thought he heard a small mew.

'Tibby!' he shouted. 'Tibby!'

'Miaow!' said a pussy-voice, and up ran Tibby to Jimmy, and purred and rubbed herself against his legs.

'Oh, dear Tibby!' said Jimmy, really delighted to see his cat again. He picked her up in his arms and made a fuss of her. She purred loudly, and then tried to get down.

'No, I'll carry you home, Tibby,' said Jimmy, and he turned to go home. But Tibby struggled very hard, and at last he had to let her go. She ran into the woods and disappeared. Jimmy was very puzzled. He went after her.

'Tibby! Why don't you want to come home with me?' he called. 'Come back! Where are you going?'

Tibby mewed from somewhere; then Jimmy saw her bright green eyes looking at him from a nearby bush! He ran up and knelt down to see where she was.

And will you believe it, Tibby was lying down comfortably in the fine new basket that Jimmy had lost when he was looking for the bird's nest! There she was, as cosy as anything, looking up at Jimmy.

But there was still another surprise for the little boy, for when Tibby jumped out of the basket, what do you suppose he saw at the bottom? Why, five beautiful little tabby kittens, all exactly like Tibby! He stared and stared and stared! He simply couldn't believe his eyes!

'Oh, Tibby!' he said, 'Oh, Tibby! I've

found you – and the basket – and some kittens, too! Oh, whatever will Mummy say!'

He picked up the basket with the kittens and set off home. Tibby ran beside him mewing. When he got home he called his mother and showed her his surprising find.

She was just as astonished as he was! 'Oh, Tibby, what darling little kittens!' she cried. 'You shall have them in your own cosy basket by the fire! Fancy you finding our basket in the woods and putting your kittens there!'

'Mummy, I needn't spend my money on a new basket now, need I?' said Jimmy, pleased. 'I can buy my tunnel with my money.'

'Of course!' said his mother. 'We will just put Tibby comfortably in her own basket with the kittens, and then we will catch the bus and go and buy your tunnel. You deserve it, really, Jimmy, because you gave up your afternoon's play with Billy to go and hunt for Tibby – and you found a basket of surprises, didn't you?'

So everyone was happy, and Jimmy got his railway tunnel after all. As for Tibby, she was very happy to be made such a fuss of, and you should have seen her kittens when they grew! They were the prettiest, dearest little things you could wish to see. I know, because, you see, I've got one of them for my own!

8

Sally Dumble's Trick

Old Sally Dumble lived in Hollyhock cottage and did all her own work, and dug and planted in her garden, too. And then one day she fell down and broke her arm, so that she couldn't do a thing, and she was most upset!

'Whatever shall I do?' she wept. 'I shall not be able to do my work now.'

Now she had next door neighbours who soon heard what had happened. One was Dame Slapdash and the other was Mother Trim.

'Oho!' said Dame Slapdash, when she heard the news. 'I'll go in and offer to do Sally's work for her. She has plenty of money and will pay me well, no doubt. I shall make a nice bit of money out of her.'

'Dear, dear!' said Mother Trim, when

her little daughter told her about Sally's broken arm. 'Poor creature! She won't be able to do her work now. Perhaps I can spare a bit of time and go in and do a few things now and then.'

So in went Dame Slapdash to see Sally and in went Mother Trim.

'I'm sorry to hear about your trouble, Sally,' said Mother Trim. 'I'll be pleased to do a few things for you whilst your arm is bad.'

'What will you charge me?' asked Sally.

'Oh, nothing at all!' said Mother Trim. 'I don't want payment for doing a bit for a neighbour in trouble! I'd be pleased to do anything I can for nothing you know that, Sally.'

'What about you, Dame Slapdash?' asked Sally, turning to her other neighbour.

Dame Slapdash didn't at all want to do anything for nothing, but she couldn't very well ask for payment after all that Mother Trim had said. And she felt quite sure that Sally would give her a nice present anyhow. So she beamed and said: 'Oh, I agree with Mother Trim, my dear. I'll do it for nothing.'

'Well, we'll see about that!' said Sally Dumble. 'Perhaps one of you could come in one day and one the next? Then I shall be well off!'

So it was arranged that Dame Slapdash should come in that day, and Mother Trim the next, and so on.

Now Dame Slapdash was a lazy worker. If she could leave anything, she would! She didn't turn the mattress when she made the bed, unless Sally's eye was on her. She didn't dust properly, but just flicked here and there. She didn't sweep the corners but left them full of dust. And she wouldn't shake any of the rugs unless Sally asked her. No – she just did the jobs as quickly and as carelessly as she could, and liked nothing better than to make herself a cup of tea and sit talking whilst she drank it.

But Mother Trim was quite different. She loved to turn the mattress each day and pat it down flat, so that it might be comfortable for Sally that night. She couldn't bear to flick round the room with a duster – she liked to go round carefully and dust underneath the clock and behind the pictures and under the vases. She always swept the dust out of the corners. And of course she shook every single rug, and would have taken up the big carpet, too, to beat in the yard, if Sally hadn't stopped her.

Sally watched the two neighbours and said nothing. She laid a little plan, as her arm got better, and she smiled when she thought of it. Soon she would be able to do her own work again. Her little trick must soon be played.

One day she played it. It was a funny little trick. She had made up her mind to pay her two neighbours for their work – but they would have to find the money themselves!

'You have been very good to me,' she said to them. 'I am very grateful. I know I said I wouldn't pay you, but I want to give you a present all the same. I will leave the money out for you!'

The next day Dame Slapdash came along to do the jobs for the last time.

She found Sally just going out. 'I've left the money for you,' said Sally. 'Good-bye and thank you.'

Off she went and as soon as she had turned the corner, Dame Slapdash looked for the money greedily. She looked on the table. It wasn't there! She looked on the mantelpiece. She couldn't see any there either! She looked on the dressing-table. None there! How cross she was!

'It's too bad!' she said. 'She's for-gotten it! Well, I suppose I must do the jobs – but I shan't bother much about them today, seeing that Sally's for-gotten to put out the money!'

So she hurried through the work, and did it very badly indeed. Then she made herself a cup of tea, and sat down to drink it. After that she went home.

Now Sally Dumble had not forgotten to put out the money – but she had hidden it! She had put five pounds under the mattress – and Dame Slapdash hadn't turned it of course – so she hadn't seen the money! She had put five pounds under the big bowl on the sideboard, which should have been moved and dusted each day – but that hadn't been done either! She had put five pounds under the blue rug by the door so that it would be found when the mat was lifted and shaken – but that hadn't been touched, of course!

The last five pounds she had put in a dark corner, so that it would be found when the corner was swept out. But Dame Slapdash hadn't done any sweeping at all!

So all the four five pounds were still in their hiding-places, untouched, and there Sally Dumble found them when she got home that night!

'So Dame Slapdash didn't do her work again,' she said to herself. 'Well, well! No work, no pay! Now I'll put a second lot of five pounds in the same places, and see if Mother Trim finds them tomorrow.'

So she put a second five pounds in each of her hiding places, so that there were ten. Then the next morning, when Mother Trim came along for the last time, Sally was just off for the day again, and called goodbye. 'I've left some money out for you,' she said with a smile. 'Take it, with my best thanks!'

Mother Trim set to work. She went to make the bed, and she turned the mattress as usual. Underneath she saw ten pounds. Wasn't she delighted!

'Boots for Peter!' she said, and tucked away the money in her pocket.

When she went to dust the sideboard, she did as she usually did and lifted up the big bowl to dust underneath it properly. And there she found another ten pounds!

'How generous of Sally,' she said,

putting the money into her pocket. 'That will buy a new dress for Mary.'

When she went to take up all the rugs to shake them, she found another ten pounds under the blue mat!

'My!' she said. 'I didn't expect all this from Sally! Just imagine it! This will buy a new jersey and knickers for John.'

And then, when she swept out all the corners, found still another ten pounds tucked away! She really was astonished this time.

'Oh, this is too generous of Sally,' she said. 'I don't think I can accept so much. Dear, dear! It would buy me a new coat!'

Now as she went home, she met Dame Slapdash and stopped to say good-day.

'Isn't Sally a generous old thing?' she said to Dame Slapdash. 'Forty pounds she gave me, for doing those few odd jobs for her whilst her arm was broken! And the way she hid it, too – under the mattress – under the blue rug – under the bowl on the sideboard – and in that dark corner of the bedroom! Sally always was one to play a trick, wasn't she! I suppose she did the same thing to you, Dame Slapdash! Well, I never expected so much return for my kind-ness!'

Dame Slapdash stared at Mother Trim and went as red as a tomato. So that was what Sally had meant when she had said that the money was left out for her!

Dame Slapdash went home without a word. She didn't like to say anything to Mother Trim, though she guessed that she had had her own money as well as hers.

'It's my own fault!' she thought, as she took off her hat. 'I could have found that money, too. It serves me right. I'm

too careless and too lazy. Well – I'm not going to crawl round and ask Sally to give me any money. I've lost it through my own fault. I'll be better in future!'

And she was. You should see her dusting and sweeping now – and as for shaking rugs, my goodness, she is even better than Mother Trim, and that is saying something! She won't be tricked by Sally another time, you may be sure!

9

Binkie's Adventures

There was once a puppy called Binkie.
He lived in a nice big kennel with his
mother and his brother and sister, Spot
and Tiny. They had a kind mistress
who gave them good meals every day,
fresh water and warm straw for the
kennel.

Outside the kennel was a nice yard to
play in, and a ball and a big rubber
bone to chew. Really it was a very
happy home for the puppies, and Spot
and Tiny were as good as gold and very
merry and bright.

But Binkie was a naughty little pup.
He was always wanting this, that and
the other, and always begging to be
allowed to go out into the big world.

'This is a dull life, Mother,' he said. 'I

want something more exciting than this! All we do is just eat and sleep, eat and sleep, and take a run round the yard. I want adventures!'

'Don't be silly, Binkie,' said his mother. 'Adventures are not always nice. You stay at home with me till you have grown bigger. One day you will have to leave me and be someone's dog. Till then be happy and contented, and enjoy each day as it comes.'

'But it's too DULL!' cried Binkie. 'I want to chase something! I want to bite someone! I want to do something really exciting!'

His mother grew tired of listening to him and went to sleep. Binkie felt cross and ran into the yard. And then he saw something that made him feel very excited. There was a hole in the wire fence that ran round their yard!

'I do believe I can squeeze through that hole!' thought Binkie, and he began to yap with excitement. He pushed and pushed against the hole, and at last, yes, he really was through it, and stood outside the yard. How excited he was! He ran off wagging his tail nineteen to the dozen.

'Now for adventures!' he thought. 'Oh, how happy I shall be to have some real adventures!'

He ran on until he came to a small field, and there he saw a great many fluffy little chicks, running about and cheeping in their high voices. 'Here is something to chase!' he cried happily,

and he ran at the chicks. They scattered at once in fright. Binkie enjoyed himself very much.

But oh, my goodness, what was this? Something big and feathery suddenly flew at him in a rage and a sharp beak pecked him hard on the nose and then on the neck, and last of all on the tail – poor Binkie turned in fright and fled away!

'Cluck-a-luck, cluck-a-luck!' cried the angry mother hen, scampering after him. 'Cluck-a-luck!'

'Ooh!' said Binkie, sitting down in a hedge to get his breath. 'What a nasty creature! She did frighten me!'

After a while he ran on again and came to a farmyard where there was a big barrel turned on its side. This made a kennel for Rover, the farm dog, who was asleep in it. Outside lay a great big bone. Binkie ran up to it joyfully.

'Now this is the sort of bone I have always wanted!' he yelped. 'What a feast I will have!'

He did not see the big farm dog in the barrel. He pounced hungrily on the bone and began to gnaw it. Rover heard the sound of teeth and opened one eye. When he saw the puppy outside, eating up his bone, he sprang up in a rage. In a flash he was out of his kennel and had

caught hold of the pup by his neck. He shook him this way and he shook him that way, and last of all he threw him up into the air. Binkie came down with a bump that knocked all the breath out of his body.

'I'll teach you to eat bones that belong to others!' barked Rover. 'Be off with you before I bite you to bits!'

Binkie fled in terror. He began to wish he was back in his own yard again. But after a while he got back his breath, and looked round boldly. He saw a man coming across a field, and he ran up to him. The man was a gypsy and when he saw Binkie, he looked at him closely, for he saw that he was a valuable little dog. 'Good dog, good dog!' he said to Binkie, and patted him. Then very quickly he lifted up the puppy, popped him into a sack he was carrying, and hurried off with him to his caravan in the next field.

He tipped Binkie out of the sack, and tied him up to a cart by the caravan. The little dog was frightened and tried to bite the gypsy. The man gave him a hard cuff and shouted at him.

'What! You'd bite me, you miserable little pup! I'll get a whip and teach you a lesson if you do that!'

Poor Binkie! He sat still after that and when a ragged, dirty dog ran up to him, he crouched back in fear.

'Don't be afraid of me!' said the dog. 'I am Tinker, the gypsy's dog. What are you doing here?'

'I ran away from my mother's kennel this morning,' whimpered Binkie. 'I wanted adventures.' Then he told the gypsy's dog all that had happened to him.

'Well, well!' said the dog, 'you've got what you wanted, haven't you? You've had plenty of adventures, it seems to me! You ought to be pleased and happy.'

'I'm not,' said Binkie, sighing. 'I'm very miserable and lonely. That master of yours says he will whip me.'

'So he will,' said the dog. 'He is a most unkind man. I wish I didn't belong to him.'

'Oh, do help me to escape!' begged Binkie, in terror. 'Please do.'

'Well, I'll bite through your string if you like,' said the dog, taking a good look round to make sure that his master was nowhere near. 'Then you must run for your life!'

The dog chewed through the thick string with his sharp, white teeth – and Binkie was free. He darted away at once, barking thank you to the dog, and ran off through the fields, glad to have escaped.

'I don't think I want any more adventures,' he thought, as he trotted along. 'I'm tired of them: I want to go home – but I don't know where home is now. I'm lost!'

As we went along, a delicious smell came to his nose. He stopped and sniffed. It was sausages cooking! Binkie ran to where the smell came from. It was coming out of a kitchen door. Binkie put his nose in at the door. There was a cook in the kitchen, and as he peeped in, she took a pan of fried sausages off the stove and popped them into a dish on the table. Then she went out of the room.

Binkie ran in at once. He jumped up on a chair and licked the sausages. Tails and whiskers, they were hot! He was just going to have another lick when the cook came back again. She saw Binkie and rushed at him in a fine temper. She caught hold of his neck and spanked him so hard that he yelped in pain.

'You naughty little creature!' she said. 'Stealing my sausages like that! You wait till my mistress hears what I have to tell her! She will lock you up in the coal-cellar till a policeman comes!'

Then she tied him up to the leg of the table and went to fetch her mistress.

Oh dear, oh dear! Poor Binkie! He shook like a leaf with fright.

'I want my mother!' he wailed. 'I want to go back home! I keep having adventures and I don't want them any more! I want to go home!'

The cook came back with her mistress

– and as soon as she saw Binkie she cried out in surprise.

'Why! It's the little puppy that our next door neighbours missed this morning! They asked me to look for him as I went across the fields today. They will be pleased to have him back!'

124

With that she picked him up, popped him into a basket and ran to the next house with him. It was not very long before Binkie was safely back in the kennel again, being licked by his mother, and stared at by Spot and Tiny.

'Oh, Mother, I'm so pleased to be back again!' wept Binkie. 'I've been chased by a hen – and shaken by a dog – and stolen by a gypsy – and rescued by his dog – and spanked by a cook.'

'My word, you have had some adventures!' said his mother, in surprise.

'Well, you always wanted them, Binkie, didn't you? Weren't you pleased?'

'Oh, no, no!' said Binkie, cuddling up to his mother. 'I'll leave adventures to bigger dogs. I want to stay at home with you. A quiet life for me, please, and no adventures at all!'

The mother dog smiled to herself. 'Adventures come quite soon enough without you having to go and look for them,' she said. But Binkie was fast asleep, and didn't hear! You may be sure he didn't grumble about a dull life after that – no, he was a most obedient, cheerful little dog, and as happy as the day was long, running about his mother's kennel-yard, and playing with his brother and sister.

10

Good old Shelly-Back!

Shelly-Back was a tortoise. He was a very big one, too, and Mary and Jack were proud of him. They always put him to bed in a box of earth each autumn, so that he might sleep soundly in the cold potting shed. Mary had made him a little blanket with his name on it – 'Shelly-Back' – and she carefully covered him up with it.

In the spring he always woke up and crawled round his box. Then the children took him out and put him in the garden. How he did enjoy the warm spring sunshine! He would poke out his little head and look up at the sun in delight.

Mary used to borrow the polish from Cook and take a duster and give Shelly-

Back's great shell a good polish, so that it shone beautifully. He liked the two children and would let them tickle him under the chin without going back into his shell.

And then one day Daddy was dreadfully cross with Shelly-Back.

'That tortoise of yours has got on to the beds and eaten all my young delphinium plants!' said Daddy, crossly. 'It's too bad.'

'But Daddy, they will grow again,' said Mary.

'Grow again!' said Daddy. 'Yes, I dare say they will – but it will take a long time.'

Then one day Daddy was angrier still.

'Shelly-Back has eaten half my pansy plants!' he said. 'Can't you keep him off the beds, you children? What's the good of my spending money and time on the garden if your stupid tortoise behaves like that? You had better give him away.'

129

Good Old Shelly-Back!

'Oh no, Daddy!' cried Jack. 'He's our only pet. We are very fond of him. We will try to watch and see that he doesn't get on the beds.'

They did try – but one day they went out to tea, and when they came back they found Daddy very cross indeed again. Shelly-Back had eaten his new young lettuces!

'Now look here, children,' said Daddy. 'I'm very, very sorry – but I'm afraid the tortoise will have to go. I'm not going to have him spoiling the garden like this. We only have a small garden and every inch is precious. Shelly-Back is doing a lot of damage.'

Mary and Jack were unhappy. They went out into the garden and looked at the tortoise. He stared up at them and moved his funny little head from side to side.

'He's a nice tortoise,' said Jack. 'I don't want to give him away. We have had him for three years now. He will grow bigger and bigger, and be a monster tortoise, I should think, if only Daddy would let us keep him.'

132

Mary bent down to tickle the tortoise under the chin. Then she gave a cry and pointed to the back of his shell.

'Look, Jack!' she said. 'He has a little hole in his shell. Suppose we thread it with string – a very long piece – and tie the other end to a post, so that he can have a good long walk round the lawn, but can't get on to Daddy's beds. Perhaps that will be all right!'

So they threaded the little hole with string and tied the other end to a post. Shelly-Back was quite happy. He walked all round the lawn, but he couldn't get on to the beds because his string wouldn't let him. Jack gave him fresh greens to eat each day, so he was very happy.

But Daddy wasn't. He kept saying that the tortoise was still eating his lettuces. 'Two or three go every day,' he grumbled. 'It must be that tortoise. He will have to go, children. I know you say he is safely on a string – but he must get loose, because every morning when I go to look at my lettuces there are a few gone.'

Mary and Jack didn't know what to do. They tied Shelly-Back up more tightly than ever, so that he couldn't possibly get loose – but the very next morning Daddy said that two more of his best lettuces had disappeared.

'I have told old Mr. Brown he can have the tortoise,' Daddy said at breakfast. 'He doesn't grow anything except grass in his garden so Shelly-Back can't do much damage there. I will take him tomorrow.'

Poor Mary and Jack! They could have cried with disappointment, but it wasn't a bit of good. Daddy wouldn't change his mind. He went off to the office as usual, and Mary and Jack went to school.

Now it happened that the next morning Daddy thought he would get up early and do a bit of gardening. So at six o'clock he got up and dressed. He stood at the window, fastening his collar, when he saw something that made him stare. It was a small boy creeping in at the back gate! Daddy

135

wondered what he was doing, so early in the morning. Then he suddenly guessed!

'He's after my lettuces!' thought Daddy. 'He's the little thief! I'll soon catch him and give him a good shaking!'

He tore downstairs, waking up Mary and Jack, who ran to the window to see what could be happening. Daddy was going out of the garden door to catch the little boy. But the small thief saw him and, his hands full of lettuces, he turned to run.

'Daddy won't catch him now?' said Jack, in excitement. 'Look, it's Billy, that naughty little boy who always calls out rude things to people? Oh, look, he's dodged Daddy, and he's running over the lawn to the front gate. He'll get away now.'

137

But he didn't get away! What do you think happened? Why, the boy ran across the lawn and didn't see the string that tied up Shelly-Back the tortoise. His foot caught in it and over he went, bump! Before he could pick himself up, Daddy had caught him and was giving him a good shaking. He made him promise never to steal lettuces again, and then sent him off, saying that he would tell his father the very next time he heard of him doing anything wrong.

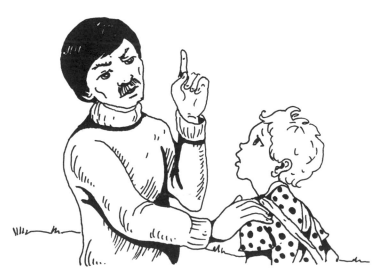

And that morning, at breakfast, Daddy said that he was not going to take old Shelly-Back to Mr. Brown.

'He wasn't the thief after all,' he said.

'But he caught the thief for you, Daddy!' laughed Jack. 'We saw him!'

'He certainly did!' said Daddy. 'Well, you can keep him. He was most useful to me this morning, and I am grateful to him because he has certainly saved the rest of my lettuces!'

So old Shelly-Back still lives with Mary and Jack. He is very big now, and his back shines as brightly as ever. If you go to tea with Mary and Jack, he will let you tickle him under his chin – but not if it's winter-time, for he will be fast asleep in his box then!

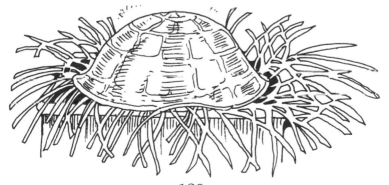

11

The Goblin and the Rocking Horse

In Janet's nursery there was a very big rocking-horse. Janet loved him, and when his tail came out and he wanted a new one, she saved up her money and bought him a lovely long one. So he was very fond of Janet and would do anything in the world for her.

'It isn't every little girl that cares enough for her rocking-horse to buy him a new tail instead of spending her money on sweets,' he said to the other toys. 'One of these days I will do something grand for Janet, see if I don't!'

Janet had a lot of toys. There were two teddy-bears, three pretty dolls, a great big panda, a pink rabbit, a black cat and a white dog. And, best of all, a fairy doll with long silver wings and a crown on her golden curls!

Janet called her Goldie-locks because of her pretty curls, and she gave her a little red chair of her own. Goldi-locks sat in it at night instead of going into the toy-cupboard with the rest of the toys. Janet was afraid that she might spoil her silver wings if she put her into the cupboard.

One day an ugly goblin came to live in the old apple tree outside the nursery window. He peeped into the nursery and made a rude face at the rocking-horse, who stood just by the window.

The rocking-horse was very well brought up, so he didn't make a rude face back. He just looked away. Then the goblin put his tongue out at the black cat.

The black cat hadn't such good manners as the rocking-horse and he put his tongue out at the goblin. It was a long tongue, and the goblin laughed at it.

'Fancy having a long tongue instead of a short one!' he cried. 'Ooh, you are a funny creature!'

'Don't be impolite!' said a silvery voice, and the goblin looked to see who spoke. It was the fairy doll, sitting as usual in her little red chair. The goblin was just going to answer rudely when he saw how beautiful the fairy doll was.

143

'My goodness me, aren't your pretty?' he said.

'Don't make personal remarks,' said the fairy doll, going red. 'And please don't come peeping into our nursery like this. It isn't nice to poke into a place that doesn't belong to you.'

The goblin disappeared – but every day he came peeping, and he tried his hardest to make friends with the fairy doll, because he thought she was so very beautiful. But she wouldn't have anything to do with him at all.

'I do wish you'd stop coming into the nursery and bothering me,' she said at last. 'I don't like you, you're very ugly, and you've no manners at all.'

'Yes, we've had quite enough of you,' said the rocking-horse, in his high, neighing voice. 'Keep away, or I may bite you!'

This made the goblin very angry indeed. He disappeared, but when he got to his home in the apple tree, he sat down and thought of a wicked plan. He would steal away the fairy doll, go to Goblin-land with her, and marry her. Then she would be his, and she would have to be nice to him.

So the very next morning he crept into the nursery as usual. He went straight up to the fairy doll and picked her up. She screamed and struggled, but she couldn't get away.

'I've got you now!' cried the goblin, and ran to the window. He didn't see that Janet was in the nursery staring at him as if she couldn't believe her eyes!

'Where are you taking my doll to?' cried the little girl frightened. 'Stop, stop!'

But the goblin didn't stop. The rocking-horse tried to nip him as he went out of the window, but he just missed him. All the toys were in a terrible fright, and as for Janet, she was so astonished that she really couldn't think what to do!

Then the rocking-horse came to the rescue!

'Jump on my back, quickly, Janet!' he cried. 'We'll go after that wicked goblin!'

147

Janet jumped on to his back, and the rocking-horse rocked out of the nursery door, down the passage and out into the garden. They were just in time to see the goblin running down the path to the bottom of the garden. After him went the good old horse, rocking for all he was worth, with Janet clinging to his back, feeling tremendously excited!

The goblin saw that he was being chased and he held the fairy doll all the more tightly and ran on fast. He raced

into the lane and then made for Bluebell Wood. A goblin bus ran through the wood every morning at eleven o'clock, and the Goblin knew that if he could

catch that he would soon be safe in Goblin-land with the fairy doll.

He ran on and on, and behind him, rocking away hard, came the rocking-horse with Janet holding tightly to the reins. The horse was panting, for he wasn't used to galloping like this, and as for Janet, she was so excited that she kept saying 'Gee-up, gee-up!' at the top of her voice. What an adventure it was!

'He's trying to catch the eleven o'clock goblin bus!' cried the horse suddenly. 'Oh dear! If we don't catch him up before he sees the bus we shall never get back our beautiful fairy doll!'

'Gee-up, gee-up, gee-up!' shouted Janet, clinging to the horse's spotted neck. On he went, rocking madly, and the goblin ran in front, carrying the fairy doll.

Suddenly Janet saw the goblin bus! It was very tiny, not much bigger than her dolls' house, and it was painted bright red with yellow wheels. The driver caught sight of the goblin and stopped his bus.

'Quick, quick, gee-up!' shouted Janet, in a fright. 'He'll get on the bus!'

The rocking-horse rocked so hard that Janet almost fell off. He raced up to the bus, and just as the goblin was jumping on, he reached out his spotted wooden neck and bit his ear!

'Ow!' cried the goblin, and clapped his hand to his bitten ear. The rocking-horse bit him on the other one, and the goblin was in such pain that he dropped the fairy doll and took out his handkerchief to tie round his head. The bus gave a jerk and went on. The goblin was on the step, trying to tie up his head, and the fairy doll was sitting on the ground crying with fright.

Janet picked her up and put her on the horse with her. The bus ran on through the wood, and the rocking-horse, now really enjoying himself, ran after it, rocking harder than ever, though he had really very little breath left! He nipped the goblin in the leg, and then nibbled seven hairs off the conductor's head. The conductor rang the bell loudly, and the driver drove so fast

that very soon the rocking-horse was left behind.

'Well, it can go!' said the horse, stopping for breath.

'We've saved Goldie-locks, and I've bitten that horrid goblin. We don't need to do any more!'

'You're a darling!' cried Janet, and hugged the rocking-horse till he neighed.

'Well, you bought me a fine new tail, and I've always wanted to do something in return,' said the horse proudly. 'Now I've done it. Get on my back again and I'll take you safely home.'

He rocked quickly home again with the fairy doll and Janet on his back; and didn't the other toys cheer him when they heard his story! Janet ran to tell Nurse – but fancy, she wouldn't believe her!

'Don't tell such silly tales!' she said. 'Whoever heard of a rocking-horse galloping after a goblin before!'

'Well, look, Nurse,' said Janet, pointing to the rockers underneath the rocking-horse: see how muddy the rockers are! There isn't any mud in the nursery, is there? So that shows he has been galloping out-of-doors with me!'

'Well I never!' said Nurse, staring. 'What an adventure you've had, to be sure!'

12

Peppermints for Grandpa Pim

Mother Pim lived in a cosy little house in the trunk of the pear tree just outside the nursery window. There was a tiny door in the trunk that opened and shut, but only the pixies knew of that.

Mother Pim had two children, Little-Toes and Twinks. They had yellow wings and pointed toes, and were very good and well behaved. They loved Mother Pim very much, and next best to her they loved their Grandpa Pim, an old pixie, who lived in an oak tree at the bottom of the garden.

Whenever Grandpa Pim came to see them, he expected to find a dish of peppermints on the table, for he was very fond of them. He came on Wednesdays and Saturdays, and on those days

Mother Pim always made sure of getting a large bag of peppermints from Tickles the grocer, who sold very nice ones indeed.

One Wednesday Mother Pim sent Little-Toes and Twinks to Tickles to buy peppermints as usual. They bought them, and were on their way home when a large brownie stopped them.

'What have you got in that bag?' he asked.

'Peppermints,' said Little-Toes.

'Give me one,' said the brownie.

'Certainly not,' said Twinks. 'They're for our Grandpa Pim.'

'Ho, that nasty old man!' cried the brownie. 'Why, he slapped me yesterday for putting my tongue out at him! Give me those peppermints! He shan't have any!'

The naughty brownie snatched the bag, and in a flash was out of sight. Twinks and Little-Toes looked at one another in dismay. Then they ran home to their mother, crying big tears of rage.

'Well, well, never mind,' said Mother Pim. 'Here is another five pence. Go and buy some more.'

But, oh my goodness, when Twinks and Little-Toes arrived at Mr. Tickles the grocer the shop was shut!

'It's early-closing day!' said Twinks in dismay. 'Oh my, now what are we to do?'

They went home again, and Mother Pim looked dreadfully worried.

'I can't think what your Grandad will say when he finds no peppermints,' she said. 'I'm afraid he will be in a dreadful rage, and perhaps he won't take you to the Queen's party on Saturday.'

157

'Oh, Mother!' cried Twinks and Little-Toes in dismay. 'Whatever shall we do?'

They sat and thought for a long time and then Twinks jumped to his feet.

'I know!' he cried. 'There's a toy sweet shop in the nursery. I've often peeped inside the window when I've been outside on the branch of our pear tree. A little boy and girl live there, and sometimes I have seen them playing with this toy sweet shop. Shall we creep in at the window when the children have gone to their dinner, and ask the little shopman there to sell us some peppermints?'

'You might try.' said Mother Pim. 'But I don't expect he has any peppermints, you know. I am sure they wouldn't be real ones.

Twinks and Little-Toes ran out of the door in the pear tree, and scampered up the branch that waved by the nursery window. In a moment they had jumped on to the window-sill, and were inside the window.

The toy sweet shop stood on the floor.

The children had been playing with it, and had left it there whilst they went to have their dinner. Twinks and Little-Toes ran up to it.

Oh, what a nice sweet shop it was! There were rows upon rows of little bottles, each with a different kind of sweet inside. There were packets of chocolate, very small indeed, and dishes of toffee – and they were all real, though very, very small!

Behind the counter stood a little shopman made of wood and cardboard.

He kept quite still and didn't move even an eyelid. But when Twinks and Little-Toes went up and spoke to him, he gave a jump.

'My goodness!' he said. 'Who are you?'

'We're Twinks and Little-Toes,' said the pixies. 'Can you sell us some sweets?'

'Well, I don't know,' said the little man puzzled. 'Do you think I ought to?

160

This shop doesn't belong to me, you know. It belongs to Peter and Nancy.'

'Well, we can give you money for the sweets,' said the pixies. 'Peter and Nancy wouldn't mind, we are sure – and besides, what is the good of having a shop if you don't sell things?'

'Very well,' said the little shopman, looking very excited. 'What is it you want?'

'Have you any nice peppermints?' asked the pixies.

The shopman looked round his shop. 'Yes, I have,' beaming all over his face. 'Look, here's a bottle full of them!'

Sure enough there was!

'We'll have five pence worth, please,' said Twinks, and he put the money down on the counter all in little brown pennies. The shopman weighed out the peppermints on his little scales, took a paper bag, and emptied them in. He screwed it up and gave it to the pixies.

'Here you are,' he said, smiling. 'My word, I do feel grand to be really selling sweets. I've only pretended before, you know. I hope you'll like the pepper-mints.'

'They're for our Grandpa Pim,' said Twinks, and off they went in a hurry, leaving the little shopman red with delight.

They arrived home just as their Grandad was sitting down in his chair by the table. He looked all round and said: 'Where are my peppermints? Don't say you have forgotten them now!'

'No, Grandpa Pim, here they are!' cried Little-Toes, and he emptied the bag into the blue dish that stood on the table.

'They look different,' said Grandpa Pim, and he took one and put it into his mouth.

'They are different,' he said, 'but my goodness, they're nice! Yes, they're very nice!'

Then Twinks and Little-Toes told him how the bad brownie had stolen the first bag they had bought, how the shop had been shut, and how they had had to go and buy some peppermints from the toy sweet shop in the nursery.

163

'Very kind of you, very kind of you indeed, to take all that trouble for your old Grandpa Pim,' said their Grandad smiling. 'You shall certainly go to the Queen's party on Saturday, and what is more, I'll buy you nice new suits to go in!'

Twinks and Little-Toes were pleased. They hugged Grandpa Pim, and tasted a peppermint each. They certainly were delicious.

But how astonished Peter and Nancy were when they came back to the nursery after dinner to play with their sweet shop again!

'The peppermints have nearly all gone!' said Nancy. 'Whatever has happened to them?'

'Perhaps someone has been buying them!' said Peter with a laugh.

'Well, that's just what has happened!' said Nancy, and she pointed to the five tiny brown pennies that the pixies had left on the counter.

'Well!' said Peter, and he picked them up and looked at them. 'Just fancy that! It must have been the fairies, Nancy, buying our peppermints – and the little toy shopman must have weighed them out and sold them!'

165

They looked at the toy shopman, and he looked solemnly back.

'You're a very good little shopman!' said Nancy. 'You did quite right to sell sweets to the fairies!'

'He winked at me!' cried Peter suddenly. 'I saw him, I saw him! Let's fetch Nurse and she can see him wink too.'

So they fetched Nurse, but the shopman wouldn't wink again.

'I don't believe it!' said Nurse. 'Such a thing couldn't possibly have happened.'

'But it did!' cried Peter and Nancy. And so it certainly had.

13

Belinda and the Bulbs

'What are we going to buy when we go out this morning, Nurse?' asked Belinda.

'We've got to go to the flower nursery and get some bulbs for your Mummy to plant in her bowls,' said Nurse. 'We shall get lots of daffodils, because Mummy is so fond of those.

'I wish she'd let me plant them for her,' said Belinda. 'I'd love to play about with that earthy stuff they plant them in, and pack it all into the bowls.'

'Well, if you're a good girl, I'll ask Mummy if she'll let you help,' said Nurse.

But wasn't it a pity, Belinda wasn't a good girl at all! She stepped right into the middle of three puddles, she rubbed her nice clean gloves in some wet paint, and she ran across the road without holding Nurse's hand.

'Well, you're just about as naughty as you can be this morning! said Nurse, crossly. 'I don't know what's the matter with you - really I don't! I certainly shan't ask your Mummy to let you help with the bulbs, Belinda.'

'Well, I shall help with them, all the same!' said Belinda rudely.

Nurse bought a big bag of daffodil bulbs and then went to the grocer's. She bought some bacon, some onions and some soap. Then she turned homewards, her basket quite full.

Belinda sulked all the way home, so Nurse said nothing to her, thinking she really was a naughty little girl this morning. When they reached home Nurse put her basket down in the hall and then sent Belinda upstairs to tidy her hair.

'You'd better sit down quietly with

your sewing,' said Nurse. 'I'm going in to ask Mummy about your new frocks.'

'I want to come too, and ask her if I can help to plant the bulbs,' said Belinda.

'Well, you can't,' said Nurse. 'You've been much too naughty. Go straight upstairs and do as you're told.'

Belinda ran upstairs crossly. As soon as she heard Nurse go into the drawing-room to talk to Mummy, she crept down again and went to the basket that Nurse had left in the hall.

'I will plant those bulbs!' she said to herself. 'I'll take them now, and get some earth from the garden. Then I'll find Mummy's four big bowls and plant them all. Nurse can't stop me if I've already done them!'

She opened a paper bag that she found in Nurse's shopping basket, and peeped inside.

'These are the bulbs!' she said. 'Good! I'll put them in the nursery, and then I'll go outside and get some earth!'

She hid the bag in the nursery, then ran downstairs and out into the garden. She filled a wooden garden basket with earth and carried it upstairs. She had to fill it twice before she had enough for the four big bowls. Then she emptied the bulbs out of the bag.

'Now I'll plant them!' said Belinda. 'Oh dear, I do hope I'll have time before Nurse comes back.'

She pushed the little brown things into the earth, and soon each bowl held about six bulbs.

'Now I'll put them in a dark cupboard, just like Mummy did last year,' said Belinda. 'Nurse will never know I've planted them – not till Mummy asks, and then won't Nurse be cross to think I've planted them after all!'

She carried them to the dark cupboard on the landing and put them on the shelf inside. Then she shut the door, ran back to the nursery, and took out her sewing. When Nurse came back, she was sitting quietly on her chair.

Mummy came with Nurse, and she kissed Belinda. 'I hope you've been a good girl this morning,' she said. Belinda said nothing, but went very red.

'Did you bring me some daffodil bulbs to plant in my bowls, Nurse?' said Mummy.

'Yes, I did,' said Nurse. 'They're here in my basket.'

To Belinda's great surprise, Nurse took a bag from her basket and gave it to Mummy. Mummy opened it and looked inside.

'Oh, they're beautiful daffy bulbs,' she said 'I think I'll plant them now, whilst I remember it. I'll go and get my bowls.'

173

Belinda stared at Mummy in surprise, as she emptied a large pile of bulbs on to the nursery table. What a funny thing. Why, she had only just planted the bulbs herself, and now here were some more!

Mummy went to the shelf where she kept her bowls, and found they were not there.

'Why, that's funny!' she said. 'Where are my bowls?'

Belinda began to feel very uncomfortable. She wished she hadn't been so naughty. What was she to say to

Mummy? Then Nurse gave a cry of astonishment.

'Why!' she said, 'where are the onions I bought this morning? I know I put them in the basket, and they're not here now. Cook specially wants them for dinner – I do hope I haven't lost them.'

'Well, I seem to have lost my bowls, and you've lost your onions,' said Mummy with a laugh. 'We are unlucky.'

Just then Cook put her head in at the door.

'Please, Madam,' she said, 'I want to put some jars of jam on that shelf in the landing cupboard, and I see there are some bowls there. May I move them?'

'Bowls!' said Mummy, in surprise. 'However did they get there?'

She went to see, and came back carrying two. Cook came behind, carrying two more. Mummy put them down on the table, looking very puzzled.

Belinda wanted to speak, but somehow her tongue wouldn't say anything. Mummy turned to Nurse.

'Here are my bowls!' she said, 'and it looks as if something is planted in them. Do you know anything about it?'

'No, I don't,' said Nurse, surprised. 'What's in the bowls, do you think?'

Mummy dug her hand into the earth – and pulled out an onion!

'Good gracious me!' she cried. 'Here's an onion! And here's another – and another – and another! Why, bless us all, the bowls are planted with onions!'

'They're the onions I bought this morning!' said Nurse, and she took them one by one from the bowls.

'How did they get there?' said Mummy, in rather a stern voice. 'Belinda, do you know anything about this?'

'Yes,' said Belinda, in a very small voice. 'I thought they were daffodil bulbs and I planted them in your bowls.'

'Well, they're onion bulbs,' said Mummy. 'Why didn't you wait to ask me if you could help, before you did this silly thing?'

Belinda didn't answer, so Nurse explained to Mummy.

'Belinda wasn't a good girl this morning,' she said; 'and I said that I should tell you she mustn't help you to plant the bulbs. I suppose she thought she would do it all the same.'

'So you went to take the bulbs out of Nurse's basket, and took the onions instead!' said Mummy. 'Well, that was a clever thing to do! Whoever heard of anyone planting onions in bowls before!'

Belinda burst into tears. She did feel such a silly girl, especially when she saw that Mummy and Nurse were laughing at her.

'I'm sorry, Mummy!' she said. 'I thought they were daffodils. Don't laugh at me any more.'

'You deserve to be laughed at,' said Mummy. 'Come here and empty out this earth and take it back to the garden.

178

Bulbs have to be planted in special fibre, not earth. You have given yourself a lot of trouble for nothing!'

Belinda did as she was told. She felt very upset, and soon she whispered to Nurse that she was sorry she had been naughty. Then she whispered it to Mummy.

'Oh, well, you've had your punishment,' said Mummy smiling. 'Look, here's one more bowl left. You shall plant real daffodil bulbs in it this time!'

So Belinda did, and felt happy again.

'Isn't it a good thing Cook didn't cook the daffodil bulbs for dinner!' she said.

'It certainly is,' said Mummy. 'But I think Cook knows the difference between daffy bulbs and onions, even if you don't, Belinda!'

14

The Fairies' Shoemaker

One very hot day Marjorie was going
down the path by the cornfield, wheeling
her doll's pram. Josephine, her doll, sat
in the pram, a dear little sunshade over
her head. Marjorie thought she looked
very nice indeed.

Suddenly the little girl stopped and
looked down at her foot.

'Something is hurting me,' she said. 'I
wonder what it is. Perhaps I've got a
stone in my shoe.'

She sat down by the hedge and took
off her left shoe. She held it upside down
and shook it – but no stone fell out.
Marjorie put her hand inside and felt all
round.

'Oh, it's a horrid, nasty nail!' she said.
'No wonder it hurt me. Whatever shall I

do? It's quite a mile to my home, and I shall never be able to walk all that way with a nail sticking into my foot. It's made a big hole in my stocking already.'

Still, there didn't seem anything else to do, so Marjorie put her shoe on again and began to walk along the path with her pram. But after a bit she stopped.

'I simply can't!' she said, with tears in her eyes. 'The nail is making a hole in my foot, now! What shall I do? I can't walk without a shoe, and if I'm late Mummy will be cross.'

She sat down and took off her shoe again. She picked up a stone and tried to hammer the nail down, but it wasn't a bit of good. It only seemed to make it worse.

Suddenly she heard a small voice just by her elbow.

'What's the matter?' said the voice.

Marjorie looked round in surprise, and saw the funniest little man. He had a long beard, and wore a pointed cap and pointed shoes. Covering his tunic

was a leather apron, and in his hand he held a shining tool.

'I've got a nail in my shoe,' said Marjorie, 'and I don't know how to walk home.'

'Well, fancy that!' said the little man, with a smile. 'You couldn't have chosen a luckier place to sit down in. You're just by my cobbler's shop!'

183

Marjorie looked where he was pointing and saw a little bench by the hedge, with scores of pairs of shoes lying about. Pieces of gay coloured leather lay on the ground.

'I make and mend shoes,' said the cobbler. 'For the fairies, of course, not for girls and boys. Shall I take the nail out of your shoe for you, or hammer it down?'

'But how can you?' asked Majorie. 'My shoe is as big as your whole shop! You haven't a hammer that would be big enough to knock my nail in.'

'Oh, that's easy,' said the cobbler, and he sang a few strange words, tapping Marjorie's shoe all the time. To her great astonishment it became smaller and smaller and was at last so tiny that the cobbler took it into his hand. He ran to his bench, sat down upon it with his legs crossed and set to work to hammer down the nail. Marjorie watched him, very excited at such an adventure. Presently the little cobbler handed her back the shoe.

'It's done!' he said. 'It certainly was a nasty nail, but I've knocked it right down now, and it can't hurt you any more. You'll be able to walk home quite all right.'

'Oh, thank you,' said Marjorie. 'Are you going to make my shoe big for me again?'

'Yes,' said the cobbler, and once more he sang strange words, tapping Marjorie's shoe all the time. It grew bigger and bigger, and at last was the same size as before. Marjorie slipped it on and buttoned it. Then she stood up.

'Oh, that's quite all right now!' she said, joyfully. 'It is kind of you, little cobbler. Do tell me something I can do for you in return.'

'Well, you might tell me what that thing is called that your doll has got,' said the cobbler, pointing to the little sunshade over Josephine's head.

'That's a sunshade,' said Marjorie. 'It keeps the hot sun away, you know.'

'Well, I certainly must buy one,' said the cobbler. 'I get so dreadfully hot, sitting out here in the sun all day long. I'm sure I shall get sunstroke one day!'

'Let me give you this one,' said Marjorie, eagerly. 'It's just the right size for you.'

'Oh no, certainly not,' said the cobbler. 'No, no, I wasn't asking you for that one, little girl. I only wanted to know what it was called, so that I might buy one for myself.'

'You shall have this one!' said Marjorie, and she took it from her doll. 'Why, I've got two more at home, every bit as nice as this, little cobbler. Do have it, just to please me. You can't think how delighted I shall feel to think of you sitting under my little toy sunshade all day long, making shoes for the fairies!'

She stuck it firmly in the ground over the cobbler's bench. He was full of delight, and sat himself down underneath it with a joyful smile.

189

'It's fine!' he said, taking up a little shoe and beginning to sew a buckle on it. 'Why, it's as cool as cool can be under this sunshade. Thank you very much indeed, little girl. It's very kind of you.

And by the way – if ever you want any shoes for your dolls, remember me, won't you? I only charge a penny a pair, and you can have them any colour you like.'

'I won't forget,' said Marjorie. 'Well, thank you very much for your kindness. I must say good-bye now, or I shall never get home!'

Off she went, wheeling her pram, leaving the little cobbler sitting under her doll's sunshade, whistling merrily at his work. 'I shall buy all my doll's shoes from him,' said Marjorie to herself. 'I'll give them a pair each on their birthdays.'

She did, – and everyone wants to know where she buys such beautiful little shoes. But Marjorie never tells them. It is such a lovely secret to keep to herself; so don't tell her I told you, will you?